Fairy Ballerina

Anna Wilson lives in Northamptonshire
with her husband, David, and her children,
Lucy and Thomas. She has two black cats
called Ink and Jet and a Labrador to match
called Kenna. She has written two picture books
and plans many more books in the future.

Nicola Slater lives in the north of
England with Dave the cat. Her work can be
seen on books and tablecloths around
the globe.

Look out for the other books in the

series

Compiled by Anna Wilson

Nina
Fairy Ballerina

Star Turn

Anna Wilson

Illustrated by Nicola Slater

MACMILLAN CHILDREN'S BOOKS

First published 2007 by Macmillan Children's Books
a division of Macmillan Publishers Limited
20 New Wharf Road, London N1 9RR
Basingstoke and Oxford
www.panmacmillan.com

Associated companies throughout the world

ISBN: 978-0-230-01538-8

1 3 5 7 9 8 6 4 2

A CIP catalogue record for this book is available from
the British Library.

Typeset by Nigel Hazle
Printed and bound in Great Britain by Mackays of Chatham plc, Kent

*For Rachael Porteus and David Pickering,
with many thanks for your insight
into a boy's life in ballet!*

Chapter One

Madame Dupré had announced in assembly that a new pupil would be joining Miss Bliss's Second Year, and now Nina and her fairy friends were flying to their studio to meet the newcomer.

"I think it's weird that someone's joining halfway through the year," said Bella.

"Why?" asked Nyssa. "*You* did!"

Nina giggled. "Yes – and you made quite an entrance, remember?"

Bella frowned. "Yeah, well . . . at least I

joined in the *First* Year. This fairy must be
something special."

Nyssa and Nina agreed that must be
true. The fairies tumbled into the studio,
noisy and chaotic as ever, but their chatting
dropped to a whisper when they spotted
the huddled group in the far corner of the
room. Miss Bliss and Mrs Wisteria were
chatting to another fairy, who was partially
obscured by the piano.

The new pupil! Nina thought. She
peered and jostled to try and get a better
look, but the newcomer was facing away
from the door.

Miss Bliss turned to the gossiping
gaggle of Second Years. As she did so,
the new pupil turned round as well,
causing the ballerinas to gasp with
surprise.

Bella was the only one who managed
to squeak out a few words. "But, you're
a – a BOY!" she stammered.

The new fairy made a big show of

catching sight of his reflection in the studio
mirrors.

"Eeek! She's right!" he shrieked, holding
his hands up to his face in mock horror. "I
am a boy! How did that happen? Someone
must have cast a spell on me!"

The class laughed – all except Bella.

"All right, that's enough, Star. Let me introduce you properly," said Miss Bliss gently.

Star winked at Bella, and Bella scowled angrily back at him. She did not like being teased, especially in front of the whole class: it made her feel foolish.

"Why didn't Miss Bliss tell us we were getting a *boy*?" Bella hissed at Nina.

Nina shrugged and turned her attention to Star. He had untidy blond hair that fell into his mischievous blue eyes. He was wearing a white T-shirt emblazoned with a silver star, dance tights and soft ballet shoes.

"I'm sorry, class," Miss Bliss was saying, still smiling at her little prank. "I should have prepared you better for Star's arrival. But I just couldn't resist seeing your faces! This is Star Fern. I should explain that we have never had a pupil like Star at the Academy of Fairy Ballet before—"

"Er, yeah, maybe that's cos he's a BOY, " Bella muttered rather too loudly.

Miss Bliss looked at her pointedly. "Will you let me finish, Bella?" Bella looked sullen. "Star has come from the Fairyland Football Squad," Miss Bliss announced to her wide-eyed pupils. "Star's coach, Mr Tarcel, wrote to ask if he could come here for a few weeks as part of an experiment for a new fitness regime. He thinks it would be an interesting way to work on Star's coordination and improve his stamina. Madame and I were intrigued, so we decided to see Star audition. He did very well indeed – so well in fact that I agreed to take him in *my* class, as he already seemed to know the basics . . ." Miss Bliss peered at Bella, who appeared to be choking. "Are you feeling all right?" she asked.

Bella's face had gone bright red – she was having trouble speaking. At last she managed to croak, "A *footballer*! In our class? You must be joking!"

Chapter Two

"Ballet's not just for girls, you know!" quipped Star. "Who's going to be your handsome prince when you're a prima ballerina if you don't let boys learn how to dance?"

"I haven't got a problem with handsome princes —" Bella snarled.

"That's enough!" said Miss Bliss, holding up her wand. "I won't have silly bickering in my class. You're going to have to get along and that's that. It'll only be for a few weeks. Star will be going back to the Football Squad soon enough."

"Thank my lucky 'stars' for that," Bella muttered.

"I think Bella needs a little convincing, Star," Miss Bliss said, smiling encouragingly. "Why don't you show us what you did in your audition?"

Star grinned, walked over to the far end of the studio and stood tall, his back extended, his neck long – he certainly stood like a dancer! He went up on to "demi-pointe", beautifully balanced, and took a few neat running steps, then leaped high into the air. He soared to the other end of the room, his legs stretched, his toes pointed. Nina stared in awe as Star landed lightly on his feet and gave a little bow.

Nina's classmates were as impressed as she was, and applauded enthusiastically.

Bella, however, was suspicious – he must have used magic, she thought. Out loud she asked, "How come you can jump like that? Even Nina can't leap that far, and she's the best in the class."

"Just a little trick I learned to get me away from tricky people," he said, winking at her again.

"Boys can often leap higher and further than girls, Bella," said Miss Bliss. "Star is

already very fit from all the football training he has been doing. He has stronger leg muscles than you, and that would help him jump further."

Bella scowled and turned away, folding her arms roughly across her chest.

He may be strong, but he's a pain, she thought crossly. He'd better stop teasing me or there's no way I'm dancing with *him*.

Unfortunately Miss Bliss had other ideas. "Star, go and stand between Bella and Nina. You will learn a lot from them."

Star joined the friends at the barre. Nina rolled her eyes as Bella stuck her tongue out at Star while Miss Bliss wasn't looking. She hoped Bella was not going to carry on being so grumpy. Much as she loved her friend, she could be very stroppy sometimes! Why was she being so mean? It might be fun having a boy in the class for a change.

"I want to see some lovely neat footwork today," Miss Bliss announced. "We are going to dance 'sur le cou-de-pied'. Do

you know what that means, Star?" she asked
the new pupil.

Star shrugged. "Something to do with
the foot, I guess. 'Pied' means 'foot', doesn't
it?"

Bella sneered and whispered to Nina,
"Not so clever now, is he?"

Miss Bliss smiled at Star and said, "That's
right. Bella – you seem to have a lot to say
for yourself today. Perhaps you can tell Star
what the phrase means?"

Bella shot Star a sulky look and
answered huffily, "Er, I think it means
. . . er, can you repeat the question, please,
Miss?"

Miss Bliss sighed and said, "The literal
translation is 'on the neck of the foot'. Now,
watch: this is a 'cou-de-pied *devant*', which
as I hope you all know by now means 'in
front'."

The teacher put all her weight on her
right leg, which she lowered into a "demi-
plié", and rested the tip of her perfectly

pointed left toe on the ankle bone of her right foot.

"Note that the left foot — the 'working foot' — is fully stretched, and the heel is pointing forward. Positions like this form the basis of many different steps. It is important to be precise—"

Bella yawned loudly.

"Bella, how rude!" Miss Bliss admonished. "Please cover your mouth. I don't need to see what you had for breakfast."

Star leaned over to Nina and said, "Did she have muesli? I think I can spot a few nuts and raisins from here . . ."

Nina tried to hide a giggle, but Bella had spotted her. "What did he say?" she hissed.

Miss Bliss lost her patience. "That's enough, Bella Glove," she snapped. "You are behaving very badly this morning. If I have any more of your chit-chat I'll have to ask you to stay behind after class."

Bella gasped. That was so unfair! It was Star who had been chatting . . .

As far as Bella was concerned, having a boy in her class was turning out to be a major disaster.

Chapter Three

The next day Miss Bliss had another surprise for the Second Years.

"I am delighted with the progress you have made in your demi-pointe work," Miss Bliss announced. "So delighted, in fact, that I persuaded Madame to let me try some work "on pointe" rather earlier than planned. Of course you will need pointe *shoes*, so I am taking you into Hornbeamster this afternoon to buy some."

The fairies shouted, "Hurray!" They had been so looking forward to dancing on pointe "like real ballerinas", as Nina said.

"Star, you're coming too," the teacher continued. "I know you're not ready for pointe shoes yet, but your flats are looking rather shabby." She pointed to his scuffed ballet shoes.

Bella loved shopping almost as much as she loved ballet, so shopping for ballet shoes was her idea of heaven. As she entered Bushel & Broomley, the shoe shop, even the fact that Star was with her could not wipe the smile off her face.

The fairies sat on some toadstools.

"We need to measure your feet to get the right fit," a shop fairy explained. "It's important to look after your feet while you are still growing."

Nina was the first to be measured. She was now a size three. The shop fairy waved her wand at the shelves and cried out:

Pointe shoes, size three,
Dance over to me!

A pair of shiny pink shoes with long pink ribbons leaped from the shelves, making a movement like a "pas de chat", as if they had invisible feet in them. They landed in fifth position in front of the shop fairy, waiting to be told what to do next.

"The outside of the shoes is covered in pink satin," the shop fairy explained. "But inside, the toes are very hard indeed. They

are packed with layers of satin, paper and a
hard material called 'burlap', all glued into
a block. Try them. Don't worry if they feel
strange to start with."

Nina felt nervous. "Will they hurt?" she
asked.

The shop fairy smiled. "They'll feel a
little hard until you get used to them. But
you've already danced in demi-pointe shoes,
haven't you?"

Nina nodded and looked at the new
shoes, hesitating.

"Remember —" the shop fairy added
— "before you dance in the shoes in your
studio, you must dip the toes into some
rosin."

"What's that?" Nina asked.

"Your teacher will have a rosin box in
class. It's made from the sap of fir trees. It's
to stop you slipping on wooden floors. It
crumbles into a white powder when you
step on it, so you leave white footprints
wherever you go!"

Nina gingerly slipped her right foot
into one of the shoes. It did feel weird. She
didn't think she'd ever be able to dance
in shoes like these. She tied the ribbons
carefully round her ankle and pulled up the
drawstrings, tucking them neatly inside the
shoe, out of sight. Then she reached down to
put on the other shoe. She tried walking in
them, pointing one foot in front of the other
as her teacher had shown her. They did feel
tight. She tried to rise up on to pointe
– and promptly fell over.

"Ow!" she cried.
"My toes!"

Bella was watching Nina, waiting to be fitted. She was feeling increasingly uneasy.

"Does it really hurt that much?" she asked anxiously.

The shop assistant smiled. "Your teacher will make sure you do all the right exercises to strengthen your feet."

Bella did not look convinced, and Nina tried to distract her while she tried on her shoes, by telling her what had happened when she had come to Bushel & Broomley with her naughty little sister, Poppy. "You know what Poppy's like. She was jealous that I was getting all the attention, so she turned some shoes into frogs! Mum was furious. But looking back, it was hilarious!"

"I bet!" said Bella, grinning. "Pity she's not with us today. Imagine the fun she'd have ..." She bent to tie her ribbons and then leaped up, screaming and flicking at her legs in panic.

"Argh!" she yelled. She was surrounded by a ring of ballet shoes that had danced off the shelves and were taking it in turns to jump up at her, turning into grasshoppers as they did so.

Chapter Four

"**A**re you sure Poppy isn't here after all?" Bella yelled.

"No – no . . . how could she be?" Nina stammered.

"What *is* all this fuss?" asked the shop fairy, coming back from fitting Nyssa. "Pointe shoes don't hurt that much – argh!" She too screamed at the enchanted shoes.

"Oh, really!" cried Miss Bliss, coming over. She flicked her wand and said irritably:

Ballet shoes, behave yourselves!
Go back to your places on the shelves!

The grasshoppers immediately changed back into shoes and tidied themselves away.

However, the shop fairy was furious. "Please keep your students under control," she complained. "I cannot have disruption like this in my shop."

Miss Bliss apologized profusely and stared hard at Bella. "I am very disappointed in you, Bella," she said slowly. "I told you yesterday that I didn't like your behaviour. What has got into you?"

"But, Miss —" Bella protested. She stopped. She had caught sight of a mop of blond hair peeping out from behind the shelves. It was Star, and he was shaking with silent laughter.

It was him! Bella thought crossly. He must have heard Nina telling me about Poppy's joke . . . She opened her mouth

again to accuse Star, but Miss Bliss did not want to hear any more.

"Sit down, Bella," the teacher said grimly. "This is my final warning: if I hear another squeak out of you, you will have to explain yourself to Madame when we get back."

There was nothing for it: Bella quietly

did as she was told. She was in enough trouble as it was.

Nina had noticed Star too. She knew she should stick up for Bella, but she couldn't help smiling. It had been very funny watching Bella leap about, surrounded by grasshoppers! And she had been so moody since Star arrived. She ought to learn to take a joke, Nina thought.

"You need to lighten up, Bella!" Nina told her friend when Miss Bliss had left them. "It's not as if *you've* never played a trick on anyone. Remember how you made the piano fly around the meadow?" she added, giggling.

However, Bella was far from amused. She turned to Nina, her wings crackling with fury. "That was different!" she hissed. "I was only trying to make you all laugh. I wanted you to like me."

"What if Star's trying to do the same thing?" Nina asked.

"Huh! He can dream on if he thinks I'm

going to be friends with him!" Bella scoffed.
"I'm telling you, if he tries any more tricks
on me, he'll regret it."

Nina sighed. She felt sorry for Star.
Once Bella had made up her mind about
something, there was no persuading her. If
she persisted in arguing with Star, it did not
look like the rest of term was going to be
much fun.

Chapter Five

The next day, Miss Bliss wanted the fairies to try their new pointe shoes.

"All the exercises are moves that we have already done on demi-pointe. Star, you can copy in your soft shoes – just don't go up on pointe. If it's too hard, I'll set you some different work."

"Like buzzing off to his smelly footy mates," muttered Bella.

Miss Bliss asked Mrs Wisteria, the pianist, to play a few bars' introduction, while the fairies faced the mirror, resting both hands lightly on the barre. Miss Bliss stood behind

them so that they could see her reflection.

"We'll start with some 'relevés' in first position," Miss Bliss ordered. "Bottoms in, tummies in. Necks long. Try not to look at yourselves in the mirror – focus on how you feel . . . That's lovely, Star! Your turnout is beautiful. Well done. Bella, remember to keep your knees glued together and push your hips out. Look at Star – he's got it right."

Bella rolled her eyes, but corrected her position.

"Now, demi-plié . . ." said Miss Bliss. "And what do we do next?" she asked the class. "Yes, Nina?"

"Well, we've always come up on to demi-pointe before," said Nina slowly. "But are we going to come on to pointe today?"

"That's right! I'd like you to try, at least. I know it will feel very strange the first time. Watch me," Miss Bliss said to the sea of nervous faces in front of her.

She held out her rainbow-coloured tutu

and went down into a
gentle demi-plié. Then,
keeping her turnout,
she pushed up
strongly on
to pointe, then
lowered herself
back into first
position without a
wobble.

"Now it's your
turn."

Mrs Wisteria
played the piano as
the ballerinas lowered
themselves smoothly into
a demi-plié. That part was
easy; what followed was not.

"Ouch!" the fairies cried,
as they tried to spring up on
to pointe.

Nina toppled over on
to Bella. Bella was already

falling, and the two friends collapsed into a heap.

"You make it look so easy, Miss!" Nina laughed.

When the bluebell rang, the Second Years had never been so relieved to reach the end of a lesson.

"That was agony!" Nyssa cried once the fairies were seated in the Refectory. Nina agreed.

Star fluttered over to join Nina and her

friends. "You know what they say," he said.
"You have to suffer to be beautiful!"

Bella narrowed her eyes and snapped,
"What would *you* know about that? You're
just a knobbly kneed footballer!"

Star answered quietly, "I do *know*
how hard you have to work to be a good
dancer."

Bella sneered. "You have no idea!
You've only been here five minutes and you
think you know it all! You have to be really

fit to be a dancer, Star – much fitter than any stupid footballer. I bet I'm stronger *and* fitter than you, whatever Miss Bliss says," she added defiantly.

Star guffawed. "Some chance!"

Bella was really angry now. "OK, let's see, shall we? Let's have a competition," she said rashly.

"Bella!" Nina said urgently. "Calm down—"

"No, I want to see just how good this boy really is," said Bella, standing up, her hands on her hips. "Meet me in the studio after supper," she said to Star. "Nina and Nyssa, you come too. You can be the judges."

"All right," Star agreed readily.

Nina and Nyssa looked at each other and shrugged.

"That's settled then," said Bella flouncing out. "See you later, Star."

Star beamed. "Can't wait!" he said.

Chapter Six

Nyssa and Nina were sitting cross-
legged on the studio floor, scribbling

on a lily pad when Bella entered, still in a very bad mood.

"Are you sure you want to do this?" Nina asked anxiously. "What if Star wins? You'll get upset, won't you?"

Bella puffed out her cheeks. "*He* won't win," she said scornfully.

Star arrived just at that moment. "We'll see!" he quipped.

Nina cleared her throat hurriedly. "Nyssa and I have made a list of exercises to test your technique and your fitness."

Bella rolled her eyes. "OK, OK. Let's just get on with it, shall we?"

Nina picked up the lily pad and read out, "Ten relevés on to demi-pointe, ten press-ups, ten pliés in second position, ten sit-ups, ten 'grands échappés sautés' – that's a jump—" Nina explained, looking at Star.

"I know!" he exclaimed impatiently.

"All right, I wasn't sure . . . where was I? Oh yes. Ten pull-ups on the bars over there—" Nina continued, nodding at the bars on the far wall, where the ballerinas did exercises to strengthen their upper bodies.

"Is that it?" Bella interrupted. She didn't like the sound of the sit-ups and press-ups. She had never been keen on those.

"No," Nyssa replied, smiling at Bella. "We'd like to see ten 'pas échappés' from fifth position too!"

Bella sneaked a sideways glance at Star to see his reaction to this, and saw he looked as confident as ever. This made her all the more determined to win.

"That's it. Bella, you start. Ten relevés, when you're ready," said Nina seriously. She was secretly relishing the role of teacher. "And remember – no magic and no cheating!"

Bella faced the mirror in first position. She did a smooth demi-plié and sprang up tautly on to demi-pointe. She repeated this ten times, concentrating hard on making the exercise look graceful, accurate and strong.

Star clapped gallantly when she had finished, and then took his place at the barre. Bella smirked. She knew she had performed well and couldn't wait to see Star make a hash of it.

But he didn't. He stood tall and strong, his turnout as beautiful as Bella's. He sprang with surprising bounce on to demi-pointe and kept his balance perfectly as he bent into a demi-plié.

Nina and Nyssa put their heads together afterwards to decide on the score. They scribbled on their lily pad before asking Bella to do ten press-ups. She

managed them, but it was hard work. Star, however, did the exercise so fast that Nina and Nyssa had to stop him from doing more than ten!

With each perfect performance, Bella grew more and more annoyed with Star.

"It looks like we're pretty well matched so far," he said generously.

Bella scowled. "We haven't done the pas échappés yet."

She gritted her teeth as she went to the barre.

I bet he won't be able to keep his balance on demi-pointe in second position, she thought as she went into a demi-plié in fifth. But she felt panic rising in her throat. What if she couldn't beat this boy after everything she had said? It would be so humiliating!

She pushed up, her toes skimming along the floor to spring from fifth to second position on demi-pointe. But she wasn't concentrating properly; all she could think of was how well Star was doing . . . With a gasp of horror, she realized that she had lost control of her feet; they were skidding away from her so fast that she could not get into second position. With a crash she landed painfully in the splits on the hard wooden floor.

Star immediately ran to help her. "Are you OK?" he cried, genuinely shocked.

Bella brushed him angrily away. "This is a stupid contest! You made it too difficult — I thought you were my friends!" she shouted at Nina and Nyssa, tears spilling on to her hot, flushed cheeks.

She flew away as fast as her wings would carry her, sobbing. At last she reached her room.

"I *hate* Star! I *hate* him! He must have put a spell on me. I've never mucked up a pas échappé like that before," she cried, thumping her pillow. "I know he's using magic . . . How else could a footballer be so good at ballet? I've got to find a way to get rid of him . . ."

An idea began to take shape in her mind. She dried her eyes, found a lily pad of pink paper and began writing in large loopy letters:

To the Fairy Football Squad

Dear Mr Tarcel,
There is something I think you
should Know about Star Fern . . .

Chapter Seven

The next day Miss Bliss suggested a break from the pointe work, much to the fairies' relief.

"Let's do some improvisation on *The Sleeping Beauty* instead," she said. "It will use your knowledge of mime and eventually some pointe work too. Princess Aurora has a famous dance on pointe at the beginning of the ballet – but, don't worry, we won't be doing that yet!" she added, seeing her pupils' worried expressions.

"I know you are familiar with the story, so I would like you to listen to this Daisy

Disc to get a feel for the music," Miss Bliss was saying. "After that, I'll divide you into groups of four . . ."

The fairies sat cross-legged on the floor and listened attentively as the dreamy music filled the studio. Nina loved lessons like this when she could let her imagination run away with her. She always found it easy to picture herself as a character in the ballet. She closed her eyes as the violins played a slow sad tune. This was the part where the prince had come to the sleeping palace and was wondering how he could possibly find his way in. In her mind's eye, Nina conjured up the twisted branches of the rose bushes, entwined around the magic castle. She could see the prince, desperately slashing through the briars. Nina saw herself as the sleeping Princess Aurora. The prince had found her . . . now he was kissing her and she was waking up . . . Now she and the prince were twirling round and round in a mesmerizing "pas de deux" . . .

"Wakey-wakey!" Bella was nudging her. "The music's stopped now, Nina. Miss Bliss is going to get us into groups."

Nina smiled, still half lost in her dream, hoping that Miss Bliss would give her the chance to be Aurora.

The teacher was directing the fairies into different areas of the studio. She called Nyssa over to Nina and Bella. "You three always dance well together," she said. "And I'm going to put Star in your group too, but no nonsense, OK?" she added, looking carefully at Bella.

Bella shrugged carelessly and said, "Of course."

The teacher left the group to decide which part of the ballet they would choreograph.

Star asked apprehensively, "Are you feeling OK today, Bella?"

"Yeah, yeah," said Bella. "It's no big deal."

"Great. Well, this should be fun. Which

character do you want to be?" he asked her, ruffling his hair.

"If you're going to be the prince, I'd rather not be Aurora, if it's all the same to you," she said airily. "What do you want to be, Nyss?"

"I'd quite like to be the Lilac Fairy who helps the prince across the lake," she said.

"Nina?" Bella asked, already knowing what her friend would say.

"Erm, well, I would love to be Aurora—"

"Fine. I'll be Carabosse, the wicked fairy. She comes back at the end of the ballet to try and stop the prince getting to the princess," said Bella, looking pointedly at Star.

"So you'll be fighting me – how appropriate!" joked Star.

Bella laughed exaggeratedly. "Yes, it is rather funny, isn't it?" she cried.

The group settled down to discuss their dance. When they got to the part

where Aurora had been woken by Prince Florimund and the couple were dancing together, Star said, "I think I should lift you, like this, Nina."
He took her in his arms and lifted her high in the air.

She was giggling and crying out, "Not so high!" when there was a crash as the studio door was flung open and a large, burly fairy in football kit came thundering into the room. He had black spiky hair, a

menacing face and muddy knees, and he
was waving a pink letter in his hairy hand.

"Oi! Star – put that fairy down, now!"
he yelled. "What do you think you're doing?
You're making a right spectacle of yourself."

Chapter Eight

There was a stunned silence.

"Who are you?" Nina squeaked as Star set her down rather too quickly.

"Let me handle this," said Miss Bliss. "Excuse me, but we are in the middle of a lesson," she said to the intruder. "Whatever you have to say to Star will have to wait."

"No way." The spiky-haired fairy smirked.

"It's all right, Mr Tarcel," said Star shakily. "I can explain—"

"Can you?" Mr Tarcel retorted. "Whoever heard of a footballer learning

BALLET! You're a disgrace to the squad, Star Fern – a disgrace to all fairy footballers," he added disgustedly. "It's a good job someone had the foresight to write to me." He held up the piece of pink notepaper.

Nina recognized the curly writing immediately. She looked over at Bella, who was staring at the floor and shuffling her feet.

Bella? But why? Nina thought, puzzled.

Miss Bliss shook her head. "I'm sorry, I don't understand. I thought Star had permission to come here as part of his training—" she began.

The footballer guffawed. "As if!" he yelled.

Star sighed and said, "I'm sorry, Miss Bliss. He's right. I came here under false pretences. It wasn't Mr Tarcel who wrote to Madame, it was me: I've always wanted to be a dancer, you see."

Miss Bliss frowned. "I think you'd better start your story from the beginning," she said sternly.

Star took a deep breath and started to explain how he had been pushed into going into the Football Squad.

"But you must be a good footballer – it's tough to get into the squad, isn't it?" asked Miss Bliss, baffled by the turn of events.

"He's one of our best!" said Mr Tarcel forcefully.

Star sighed. "Oh, I'm good at running

fast, and my footwork's neat ... But I
don't love it like I love ballet!" he cried
passionately. "I want to be a dancer. I dream
about it all the time – even when I'm
running around the pitch ..."

Mr Tarcel snorted.

"But that doesn't explain why you are so
good at ballet," exclaimed Miss Bliss.

"Yeah, well, that's cos he uses magic,
doesn't he?" Bella butted in.

"I do not!" Star protested. He sighed.
"Listen, I'll tell you the truth ..."

He took a deep breath and explained
how, one day, after a particularly gruelling
training session in the gym, he had lingered
in the changing rooms. All the other players
had gone home.

"I was packing my kitbag when I heard
some wonderful music drifting out from the
sports hall next door," he said. "I wandered
over and had a look through the window. A
ballet lesson had started!"

Star soon discovered that this class

happened every week after his training session. The class used the sports hall because they had nowhere else to go. Star started watching them through the window every week and was soon hooked.

"I started copying them –" he went on – "joining in the lesson without anyone knowing! But of course eventually I was discovered. One day the teacher came out of the building because she had heard a noise outside – I had tried a difficult jump and had fallen into some dustbins! She tried to chase me away because she assumed I had been up to no good. But it was such a relief to be found out, so I explained why I was there. She still thought I was lying. She made me come into the class and dance in front of everyone."

"Serves you right," said Mr Tarcel. "Bet you felt like a right ninny."

Star shook his head. "No, I didn't! I felt happier than I had for months! The teacher asked if I wanted to join her class.

I explained that my
family would have a
fit if they knew I was
doing ballet—"

"Of course
they would, mate!"
scoffed Mr Tarcel.

Star ignored him
and continued. "She
said she thought it
was a shame. In the
end she agreed to
let me have free
lessons and not to
tell my family, because she said I showed
potential."

"How did you hear about the
Academy?" Miss Bliss asked. She was
stunned. This was too much to take in.

"My teacher mentioned it," Star
answered. "She said you had taken boys in
the past. There is no academy for boys, is
there?"

Miss Bliss shook her head. "Boys usually have private lessons. Not enough boys do ballet to set up a boys' academy, unfortunately," she said.

"That's why I had to fake the letter," Star finished. "My family would never have written it for me. It was the only way I was going to get my wing in the door . . . and the only way I might persuade the Academy to let me stay . . ."

Star stopped and looked pleadingly at Miss Bliss.

Nina's heart was beating fast. She couldn't bear it if Star had to go back to the squad. How could the Academy be persuaded to let him stay?

Chapter Nine

Bella was touched by Star's story. She had only wanted to get Star into trouble with his coach by saying that he had been using magic to cheat in his training. She'd had no idea that Mr Tarcel hadn't even known Star was at the Academy in the first place! She remembered only too well how it felt to be pushed into doing something she didn't want to do – her mother had sent her to the Jazz Dance School, and she had hated that. She had run away to the Academy herself! She admired Star for finding a way in to the ballet school.

"It was clever of you to fake that letter," said Bella. She blushed. "In fact, you're not the only one to have written a letter you shouldn't have," she admitted.

Miss Bliss's face looked like thunder. "Bella! How could you? I know Star pulled the wool over our eyes, but—"

"It's all right," said Star quickly. "I'm glad it's all out in the open. But, please, Miss Bliss – do I have to go back to the squad?"

Miss Bliss frowned. "I must admit that seems a bit harsh. Mr Tarcel and I will have to talk to Madame . . ."

Mr Tarcel was dumbfounded. "If your heart's not in the footy, mate, I don't want you back," he said. "But I don't know what your family's going to say. They don't know you're here, do they? I only found out because of that young fairy's letter. I thought you'd gone home because your granny was ill!"

"I know," Star admitted. "I faked another letter to Mr Tarcel from my mum and dad," he explained to Miss Bliss. "I figured that way the squad wouldn't contact them when they found me missing."

Miss Bliss sighed. "So you lied to me, you lied to your family and you lied to Mr Tarcel?" she said quietly.

Star nodded dumbly.

"I do not approve of lying under any circumstances," she said. "But I do agree that you show enormous potential as a ballet dancer. And I am very keen to keep you with us, but I cannot do that unless your family and Madame Dupré agree." Despite the teacher's serious expression, Nina thought she could detect a glint in her eye.

Star stared at his feet.

Bella suddenly jumped into the air and waved an arm about excitedly.

"What is it now, Bella?" Miss Bliss asked irritably.

"I've had an idea!" Bella cried.

Star looked at her nervously.

"Yes?" said Miss Bliss.

"Why don't we invite Star's family here to watch him dance!" she said, her almond eyes shining at the idea.

"You've changed your tune!" cried her teacher in astonishment.

Bella blushed. "Yes, well, I didn't realize how important ballet was to Star until today. I know how it feels to be pushed into doing something you don't want to do . . ." she added with passion. "I think Star deserves the chance to explain how he feels to his family, and the best way of doing that is to show them what a great dancer he is."

Miss Bliss nodded approvingly. "Bella, I think you just might have the solution," she said.

Star yelled, "Yippee!" and threw his arms round Bella.

Bella smiled weakly, relieved that she had been able to do something to make up for her unfriendliness.

Chapter Ten

adame Dupré agreed that Star should perform to his parents.

"In my experience, actions speak louder than words," she said wisely. "If Star gives a stunning performance, his family is sure to understand his passion."

Miss Bliss decided everyone should be involved in dancing the last scene from *The Sleeping Beauty*. It was agreed that Nina would play Aurora; Nyssa, the Lilac Fairy; Bella, the wicked fairy Carabosse, and Star, Prince Florimund. The others would be the

palace staff who had fallen under Carabosse's spell.

On the night, they changed into their costumes in silence. They had not had much time to get ready for this performance, and everyone was nervous.

"You all look fantastic!" Miss Bliss reassured them, coming backstage before the curtain went up. "I just know you won't let Star down!"

Star was quaking in his ballet shoes as the fairies took their places behind the curtain. He had peeped out earlier and spotted his mum and dad in the front row. They had looked very unhappy. What if they caused a scene and dragged him offstage?

The lights in the Grand Hall went down; the chatter in the audience was reduced to a murmur; the stage lights went up; the curtains swished back . . .

A beautiful scene of a palace hung on the back wall of the stage, and a very realistic

Star Turn

boat sat stage left. Hazel had found it – it had been used years ago for a performance of *Swan Lake*. Tonight it was to be the Lilac Fairy's boat in which the prince would escape from the evil Carabosse.

In the middle of the stage was a four-poster bed draped with silk curtains. On the bed lay Nina as the beautiful Princess Aurora. She was dressed in a delicate pink gown with silver stars. Her arms were hanging limply at her sides, her long blonde hair was brushed so that it fanned out on the pillow, framing her face. All around her, other characters from the ballet lay sleeping. Hazel was dressed as the princess's little dog, sound asleep at the foot of the bed!

Miss Bliss pressed the "Play" button on her Daisy Discplayer and the music swirled out, filling the Grand Hall. Star pirouetted on to the stage, dressed as the prince, in a silver outfit. Nyssa, clothed in lilac, ran to meet him on demi-pointe and gestured to

him to get into the boat with her and sail
across to the enchanted palace.

But they were stopped by Bella as
Carabosse, who whirled on to the stage in
her dramatic black costume, her arms lifted
above her head to make her look menacing.
Both Nyssa and Bella used dramatic mime
to show the audience that they were

engaged in a magical battle: Carabosse
desperately tried to stop the Lilac Fairy from
helping the prince, but in the end the Lilac
Fairy's magic was too strong, and Carabosse
slunk away, defeated. Bella crouched down
low and danced off the stage backwards, on
demi-pointe.

Star then mimed a great struggle through
the briars that bound the palace. He broke
through at last, making his way to Aurora's
room. When he saw the princess asleep,
he stopped dramatically to gaze upon her
beauty. Then, bending his left leg in a demi-
plié and stretching out his right leg, his foot
pointed, he gracefully stooped to kiss Aurora.

The princess awoke. She lifted her head,
and saw the prince looking at her. His face
full of joy, he swept her up into his arms and
danced to the front of the stage, holding her
high above his head!

The audience rose up from their seats,
fluttering in mid-air, clapping, cheering and
whistling even before the dramatic music

had finished. Star gently set Nina down and she beamed at him as they made a curtsey and a bow.

"If that doesn't convince them, nothing will!" she cried above the din of the applause.

Star nodded, tears in his eyes. He had never dreamed he would get the chance to dance before his mum and dad, least of all on a stage with other dancers.

When the applause had died down, Miss Bliss came to the front of the stage and presented Star with a bouquet of wild flowers. Then she turned to face the two fairies in the front row.

"Mr and Mrs Fern," she said. "I hope now that you will see what a talent your son has. I would like you to know that the Royal Academy of Fairy Ballet believes that Star has a great future ahead of him – as a _dancer!_" she emphasized.

Star's mum and dad could do nothing but nod. They had been moved to tears

by their son's performance and were still dabbing at their eyes with their handkerchiefs.

The applause started up again as the curtain finally fell on the stage.

Bella ran over to Star and hugged him, beaming with happiness. Then, standing up on the tips of her toes, she cried out above the whooping and cheering of the audience:

"Star Fern – you really are a STAR TURN!"

Log on to

Nina
Fairy Ballerina
.com

for magical games, activities and fun!

Experience the magical world of
Nina and her friends at the Royal
Academy of Fairy Ballet. There are
games to play, fun activities to
make or do, plus you can learn more
about the Nina Fairy Ballerina books!

Log on to www.ninafairyballerina.com now!

Fairy Stories

Chosen by Anna Wilson

Every fairy has a story to tell

Be spirited away to fairyland and visit the wonderful worlds of dream fairies, funny fairy godmothers, a sweet-toothed cake fairy and a fairy who learns a lot about friendship.

This magical story collection is a must for all fairy fans.

Princess Stories

Chosen by Anna Wilson

Every princess has a story to tell.

A pretty perfect princess and a badly behaved princess, a princess in love and a princess in BIG trouble . . .

These are just a few of the princesses on parade in this fun, magical story collection.

A selected list of titles available from Macmillan Children's Books

The prices shown below are correct at the time of going to press. However, Macmillan Publishers reserves the right to show new retail prices on covers, which may differ from those previously advertised.

ANNA WILSON

NINA FAIRY BALLERINA

New Girl	978-0-330-43985-5	£3.99
Daisy Shoes	978-0-330-43986-2	£3.99
Best Friends	978-0-330-43987-9	£3.99
Show Time	978-0-330-43988-6	£3.99
Flying Colours	978-0-330-44622-8	£3.99
Double Trouble	978-0-330-44620-4	£3.99
Party Magic	978-0-330-44778-2	£3.99
Dream Treat	978-0-330-44780-5	£3.99
Star Turn	978-0-230-01538-8	£3.99

CHOSEN BY ANNA WILSON

Fairy Stories	978-0-330-43823-9	£4.99
Princess Stories	978-0-330-43797-4	£4.99

All Pan Macmillan titles can be ordered from our website, www.panmacmillan.com, or from your local bookshop and are also available by post from:

Bookpost, PO Box 29, Douglas, Isle of Man IM99 1BQ
Credit cards accepted. For details:
Telephone: 01624 677237
Fax: 01624 670923
Email: bookshop@enterprise.net
www.bookpost.co.uk

Free postage and packing in the United Kingdom